# Three Dimensions

# Three Dimensions

Lizzies Fizzies

ELIZABETH REINACH

To order additional copies of this book, contact:
Xlibris
800-056-3182
www.Xlibrispublishing.co.uk
Orders@Xlibrispublishing.co.uk
799885

# BOOBY PRIZE

Before 1930, brassieres were not known. Binding of the breasts was often done to ensure a silhouette line, or a camisole was worn over the whole body. Underwired brassieres were worn for the first time in 1928, to raise and separate the breasts. The triangular cups were sized A to G. The brassieres could be specially commissioned from an underwear maker or bought from Marks and Spenser or Selfridges.

The Church Rest was a hotel in north London dedicated to making Anglican clergy comfortable during their visits to the capitol. Bradley had been a butler at Church Rest for twenty years. The maid, who had been cleaning out the room which the bishop just vacated, handed Bradley a number of brassieres she had found underneath the pillow. Neither knew what they were, but Bradley guessed they related to women's anatomy. He took the bras from the maid, and cut them through the front fastening, and undid the back clasps.

The bras were made of tulle, silk, or satin with lace decorations. Bradley piled the half bras up in his Butler's pantry and locked the door.

\*    \*    \*

The Reverend Henry Mount, Vicar of St Joseph's in Sudwell, had come up to London to sort out a bit of bother, staying as usual at Church Rest.

He had eaten a substantial dinner and was now relaxing in his favourite arm chair. The dinner had been excellent, but the pudding on offer was poor—rice pudding, fit only for the nursery, no gateaux or fruit. He motioned for Bradley to come over and asked him if there was a ripe apple in the kitchen.

With his usual air of subservience, Bradley went to look. He returned promptly and dangled an apple in a red satin cup. It was decorated with white lace, and hung from a latex band.

'Oh this is nice. What a pretty container. Is this how fruit is served in London, Bradley?' said Harry.

'I believe so, sir,' said Bradley, bowing.

Jeremiah Steed, a canon at Westminster Cathedral, had escaped to Church Rest away from his ecclesiastical duties and was relaxing in the lounge. He recognized Henry Mount, known to be a frivolous man and often not far from trouble. He noticed he had fruit in a lace container, and was just about to turn his back on Mount, when he was seized with a desire for an orange. He called to Bradley, and asked for an orange, in a pouch like the other clergyman was twirling around.

Bradley returned with an orange in a larger pouch than the one the Rev Mount was holding. The pouch the canon was given was dark green with black lace trimmings. The canon saw Mount watching him.

Mount came over. He looked at the orange swinging in the pouch.

'Exotic, or is the word "erotic"?' said Mount with a laugh.

The canon looked away in distaste.

'Bradley come here,' shouted Mount. 'Why are these cups of different sizes? How many sizes are there?'

Bradley said, 'The size letter is attached to the seam. A to G. Yours is B, the Canon's pouch is D.'

'What, for different-sized fruits? And what's the G for? A melon or pineapple?'

'Probably, sir.'

'And where do you buy them? My mother would like some.'

'Your mother would serve fruits in these things?' said the canon with disgust.

'As they have found favour with you, I shall order some more from Selfridges today. There will be a large party in the lounge tomorrow, coming from the Conference. Our Ministry moves to Life on the Streets. They will use the lounge in Church Rest,' said the Butler.

'And enough fruit too, Bradley, don't forget. We want to fill the bigger cups.'

The kitchen staff squeezed big fruit, melons, and pineapples into G and FF cups. Pears and oranges were slung into C and D cups; and little fruits, tangerines and plumbs, into A and B cups.

The young clergy came in from the conference and seized the colourful pouches spread out on the table. There was much genteel merriment. Once the pouches were filled with fruit, 'conkers' was played, and a large melon was defeated by a small apple in a 'David and Goliath' contest.

'If you want to play,' said the canon, 'go on the Heath. You will spoil the nice furniture in here. There is an esquitorial from Bishop Howard and Turkish carpets donated by Anglican travellers.'

'A cup and fruit race!' said Henry, 'On the Heath. Come on brothers. Get your fruit.'

'If you want to play,' said the Canon, 'why don't you get out of here and go on the Heath? Bradley won't want you damaging grabbed fruits and cups.'

The clergymen, still wearing their cassocks ran like a group of excited black birds, flapping out of the door.

Henry Mount said, 'Some of you are cheating. You have taken the small fruits. The ones with the melons will be weighed more down for the race. They should have a handicap of one hundred yards.'

The racers organized themselves in lines—the melons and pineapple bearers at the front, the plumbs in their tiny cups at the back.

Walkers on the Heath started to gather to watch the clergy race. As a result of a tip-off from Clergy Rest to the ever-manic Mr Selfridges, a tent had been pitched at the end of the track; on it was a poster saying *Booby Prize*.

Some of the clergy fell over their cassocks, and some lost their fruit. The children playing on the Heath laughed.

Henry Mount was the clear winner carrying pear DD.

The clergyman who fell first was the Canon, carrying pineapple FF.

Both the winner and the Booby were asked to come forward. A man, who was obviously the well-known retailer Mr Selfridges, came out of the tent and beckoned the clergymen towards the tent where he could greet them.

'Reverend Henry Mount, the winner, has a bottle of champagne, whereas Canon Steed has the booby prize.' Out of the tent stepped a beautiful model. She wore a long, blue shimmering evening skirt, and on top, only a black silk bra with gold appliqué. Whispers said the bra was DD.

Mr Selfridges's staff were shouting on loud speakers advertising the department in Selfridges in which the new women's underwear could be bought and a roar of appreciative laughter came from the clergymen. Mr Selfridges gave his sales pitch for his department store with details of fitting times and prices.

Henry Mount, whose eyesight was acute, could just see the ample figure of the bishop moving about in Mr Selfridges's tent.

# FLAMBOYANT

Two birds, black hawk and vulture, conferred over a testimonial.

'Look,' said Hawk, pointing to a word 'flamboyant'. 'Mr Stone says Mr Brown is "flamboyant". What does he mean?'

'He can't mean that he's a . . .,' said Vulture, peering at the word.

'Ah, no, no, surely not, not a . . .,' said Hawk, as he peered more closely at the word as if it would give away its secret. 'No, surely not. Anyway, it says under *Personal* that Mr Brown is married, so he's not a . . .'

'Perhaps, its women then,' said Vulture.

Hawk was longing to meet Mr Brown.

'He knows Excel, has managed staff. I think we should offer him an interview.'

'Oh yes,' said Vulture. 'Here in the Board Room. We could interview him here. We've had all types in here.' He sniffed the lingering smell of perfume.

\* \* \*

The interview was to be held on Wednesday. Hawk put on a red spotted tie. He smelt danger in the air while he ate his croissants. *Gaie Paris*, he thought.

'Have a good day,' his wife said, smirking, as he left.

*She knows*, he thought as he got into his car.

Vulture stood before his mirror, a game smile on his face, while he trimmed his moustache. He flicked a green handkerchief into his pocket, like a magician doing a conjuring trick.

Hawk and Vulture waited tensely in the Board Room, for the footsteps of the secretary, bringing in the candidate. She ushered in a small drab man.

He answered all the questions precisely and politely, without any trace of anxiety.

'And what do you do with your free time?' said Vulture, 'Anything out of the ordinary?'

Hawk and Vulture leaned forward to hear the least hint of 'flamboyance'.

'My wife and I usually hear TV in the evening. We have a dog. We go for walks with him.'

'Anything else?' Vulture's eyes were bulging.

'Well no,' said Mr Brown, confused by the onslaught. He pushed his chair back and started to stand up.

They gave him the job, and Mr Brown joined the Bank. He fused into the bureaucratic machine like a tidy cog. Everything he said and did seemed orthodox; everything was as satisfactory as Bank procedures. He was polite and friendly to all his male and female colleagues, but never had a familiar manner.

Hawk and Vulture sometimes spoke of him.

'He's a dull dog.'

'He's a drab mouse.'

And they felt cheated.

At the end of the month, when the reckoning was done, Hawk and Vulture went to the Judge's Wig for a drink of port. They met Mr Stone who was the Voice of the rival bank who had sent the testimonial for Mr Brown.

After the formalities and best wishes, Hawk asked Mr Stone why he had said that Mr Brown was flamboyant.

'He's a dull dog,' said Vulture.

'He's a drab mouse,' said Hawk.

'Why did you say it?' they said together.

'He was out of line. We all vote Conservative at the Bank. He voted Labour.'

'He's a revolutionary,' said Hawk ecstatically.

'A Revolutionary!' said Vulture.

# GREEN AND LARK

The dried grass swayed in the vase on the wooden table. The roof was low, and the kitchen equipment shone red in the gloom of the gathering dusk. Mrs Green switched on the overhead light and took the meat out of the oven. The strong smell of baked animal filled the kitchen.

'Come on, supper!' she shouted up the stairs.

Her son swung on the banister. Her young daughter, standing on the stairs, kicked him. Her husband entered by the front door in his brown mac. The family hunched together round the kitchen table. Mrs Green ladled food from an iron pot.

Dawn, the 13-year-old daughter, jumped up and down on her chair.

'Simon's growing a tail!' she cried out. 'He'll be like Zac—two doggies wagging their tails together. Will it be a brown tail?' she turned to ask her brother. 'Long and thin? Will you swing from the trees with your tail?'

'Shut up, Dawn. Eat your supper,' said her mother, but Dawn continued.

'Andy says he knows Simon's growing a tail. Andy felt Simon's spine. He knows a tail is growing. Andy says Simon should grow his hair long, now that he is getting to look like an animal. Come on, Simon, brush my hair. Andy says—'

'Andy says, Andy says . . . Do we have to hear anymore?' said Mr Green. Andy Lark was his business partner's son, so he had to tolerate his friendship with his children; but they saw more of him than their father wished. What he did to preserve good relations at Green and Lark, Solicitors!

Two days later the Green parents and Simon were eating peanuts hunched round the television in the snug. Dawn burst in.

'Andy says I'm turning into an ape. I told him I was growing hair on my body. Andy says Simon and I are both turning into apes.'

'Now, Dawn, you know what happens at puberty to boys and girls. You shouldn't talk to Andy about your body. It's very rude to talk to a boy like that. If you are worried about your body changes, you can see Dr Oldman if you wish,' said her mother.

'Andy says—'

'We don't want to hear what Andy says, and don't swing on the door. Come and share some nuts with your brother.'

Stephen Green wished he had the courage to confront his partner, Jeremy Lark, about the children's friendship, but Jeremy's very humour was a barrier. He was grinning when Stephen approached him at the office the following day.

'I think this is a suitable project for you to get your teeth into. If you agree, I'll send the project brief to you. We've been asked to put forward the case for a planning objection by a Conservation Lobby against *New Build,* who, as a petitioner claims they have a Right to Build on that part of the Green Belt. You will have to defend the rights of all those furry animals with tails, whom the Conservation Lobby hold most dear.

'And you think that suits me? Andy said....' Stephen Green's words petered out

'Come on, Stephen, you'll make a great job of it, with your history,' said Jeremy Lark.

'History?' said Stephen.

'Come on, you'll make a good job of it, and we'll get more of this kind of work. The Forestry Commission have offered to take you on a trip around the site tomorrow.

Stephen Green was led through the site by Objectors and was asked to put on brown Forestry Commission overalls. On a strange impulse he stretched out his brown clad arms and reached for the trees. An 'objector' brought out a folding ladder and helped Mr Green up. He swung gently from the tree boughs. Ten thousand years of pungent foliage assaulted his nostrils. He looked down, perfectly at home, as he swung from tree to tree as if to the melody of a song.

'I can see the wonder of the forest from here,' he said. A camera's lens flashed.

Stephen Green felt he could write the objector's case fluently, the glories of the woodland, its place in sustaining life, the rights of creatures, big and small.

Jeremy approved Stephen's report, and put the picture of Stephen swinging in the trees on the front cover.

'That gives a homely hands-on impression.'

He added, 'We can also put the picture in the window of the Solicitor's agency, with the "properties for sale".'

Stephen was invited back to the forest by the objectors. He went there often now, with his family, and Andy Lark.

Usually at lunch time, Jeremy and Stephen went to The King's Head, a beamed seventeenth pub, where the decapitated head of King Charles hung outside, but today Jeremy had to go to the dentist, as he put it, 'his nashers were not noshers'.

Stephen ate a sandwich in the office, then he went down the High Street to take a look in the bookshop.

Andy Lark was inexplicably at the door.

Amongst the 'Two for the Price of One', a dust jacket caught his eye. It showed a family of four apes, doing what appeared to be an obscene dance. A hand came from behind him and took a copy of the book. Another hand came from the other side and took another copy. Out of the corner of his eye, he could see Andy pointing in the direction of the pile, while he talked to customers.

A queue was forming at the checkout, most had a copy of the book, *The Ape Family.*

Stephen sneaked a fearful look inside the book. On the dust cover, it said, 'the story of an ape family of limited intelligence and how they managed to overcome disadvantage.' The book was styled 'A parable of free enterprise in limited environmental and cerebral conditions—a lesson for all those planning for the underclass.'

The author was apparently a Mr Pemble, but no details about him were given on the back flap.

A man in a leather jacket came up to him.

'Will you sign my copy of *The Ape Family* please?'

'I beg your pardon. What on earth would I do that for? Are you Pemble? Who is Pemble?'

'No, sir. I saw your picture on the door of *Green and Lark.* The boy over there says the book's about you.'

'Andy! I shall phone the publisher. Who are these people? It says *Optimum Scientific Publication* on the back. Right, they're for it.' He got out his smart phone and traced the telephone number. A crowd had gathered around him.

'What is this book you have published *The Ape Family?* Who is this Pembleton who wrote it? I will sue you, do you hear? It's about my family.'

'You are going to sue us about one of our books? I know it, a very distinguished study, what is your name?'

'I'm Stephen Green, a solicitor at Applethorp.'

'We know nothing about you. It is often a guilty conscience which leads people to read themselves in books. We suggest you . . .'

At this point, Jeremy Lark ambled into the shop, and an irate Stephen Green turned on him, while the publisher was still talking.

'These people think this book *The Ape Family* is about my family.'

'Well, OK, but what with that and your work for the Conservation Lobby we have had thirty new inquiries for our services today. I was beginning to think we would go bust with the Legal Aid work drying up. Now we have Forestry Commission, Animal Charities, the lot.'

Stephen's look was visceral. He advanced towards his partner.

'Are you Pemble? Did you write that book?'

Jeremy's smile was enigmatic. He looked down at Stephen.

'Look at your hands. They're growing hairs.'

At that point, Simon and Dawn came into the shop, swinging each other's hands. Simon's hair was long now, and Dawn brushed it with her fingers.

'Daddy, come and dance with us . . .,' she said.

# KISS AND TELL

'Good Lord, what's the time?' Lord March jerked himself up on the sofa. 'What did you say?' he said to his companion. 'Tell me before I go.'

Lord Marsh disentangled himself from the limbs and ample bosom of his fellow delegate to *The Conference on the Future of the Euro*. He turned. His large stomach now confronted her. She patted it.

'What did you say?' he repeated. 'I must have dropped off. The drinks were probably spiked.'

'Well', she said, 'you found a nest in my bosom. I have told you the whole story. Little bird, tweet, tweet. No one else has been told. The story could bring down the financial world and your Government.' Her ample rear disappeared, much to his regret.

*Bring down the Government*, he mused. *Bring down Tom, who was now PM*. Tom, the sneak, the school telltale now might leave his office in disgrace. Lord Marsh rubbed his hands, anticipating glee. If he knew what this scandalous secret was, he could suggest the TV shows invite him, Lord March, to comment. He would play the hypocrite, say it wasn't in Tom's character to lie, that he had known him as a schoolboy, that he would never be deceitful. Then a sting in the tail, he would add with a smile, 'We all have our little vices, little peccadilloes, don't we?'

To anticipate Tom's fall, he must find out what the secret was, the secret the lady had whispered in his ear as he lay in her arms. Oh, to lie in her arms again and find out more, to feel her bosom pressed against his chest.

But he did not know her name. First, he must find out who she was.

Lord March strode to the reception desk in the foyer, opposite the sofa where he had lain serene and drunk in the lady delegate's arms. He pulled his tie into place, adjusted his shirt and belt, and in a voice honed at Eton and Oxford, he said,

'Tell me, woman, the name of the lady delegate I was talking to on the sofa over there. She has vital statistics, I mean information, which I must clarify, and pass on to Tom or not, as I see fit for Great Britain.'

The receptionist, who was tall, intelligent, and well informed, went red and said,

'Lord March, you seemed so friendly with the lady, surely you know her name.'

'Of course, I do, but remind me, so many foreigners here, you know.'

'She is Frau Muller, the Representative from the Deutsche Bundersbank. She is on your Conference List.'

'She said she knew a secret which could bring down the pound.'

The official sighed. 'Rate fixing. I expect. They are all at it. Euro against dollar and pound. Devaluation. Government floundering. General Election. UKIP win.'

*Tom out,* added Lord March to himself. *Tom implicated in rate fixing. Ha ha.*

'Where is Frau Muller staying in London?' he said out loud.

'Oh, I can't tell you that,' said the receptionist. 'The conference organizer, Richard Hinde Smith might tell you, if your motives are professional. He saw you on the sofa . . .'

Lord March marched to the tannoy system, and summoned the conference organizer in loud, demanding tones. The young man, ruffled and unwilling, approached.

'I am Lord March. I want to know where Frau Miller from the Bundesbank is staying.' Lord March towered over his victim.

'Sorry, sir, we can't give out confidential information about delegates. It would be improper.' He gave Lord March a piercing look and added, 'Most improper.'

Lord March said, 'She is to give me important information, about banks, that kind of thing. As a British man, your failure to cooperate makes you a traitor.'

'Rate fixing, I suppose,' replied Hinde Smith wearily. 'OK, she's at the Savoy. Don't involve me.'

Lord March's face was hard as he went through the swivel door, and he pulled his belt over his stomach. His car was waiting. The chauffeur was reading *Men's Health*. Full of testosterone dreams, he swerved off to the Savoy.

At the Savoy, Lord March was surprised to be greeted so familiarly by the receptionist.

'Frau Muller is on the fourth floor, Suite 402.'

'Is she expecting me?' asked Lord March, surprised

The receptionist smirked. Lord March pulled up his belt.

Lord March expected Frau Muller to answer the door at Suite 402, and was shocked to see a man open the door, an obvious foreigner, with an offensive foreign haircut. He linked arms with Lord March and drew him inside, where two more men were sitting on a sofa.

The man with an obvious American accent got up and held out his hand. 'Hi, Lord March,' he said. The other man, seemingly an Italian, stared ahead of him on the sofa.

'What is this?' said Lord March. 'I came to meet my special friend Frau Muller to talk about international finance.'

'Special friend!' said the Italian. 'She is my special friend. She has a secret to tell me.'

'Rate fixing,' said the Frenchman who had answered the door. 'It's always rate fixing, what a bore. I hope she whispers that she loves me, not talk about rate fixing.'

'Where is she?' said Lord March, the leader. 'Why isn't she here? Why have we all been tricked to come here?'

'She's in the bedroom fixing her bra,' said the Frenchman.

Frau Muller emerged in a silver evening gown, sprinkled with pearls and carrying a wand of gold.

'After the Ball, in the English Fairy story, the Prince wanted to find the girl he had fallen in love with. The girl had left her shoe at the Ball. The Prince wanted to find which girl's foot fit the shoe,' Frau Miller said to the waiting men.

'I am a grown up Princess. I want to find the man whose body is moulded to my figure, a mouth that fits mine. Then I will tell him my secret.'

'Rate fixing?' said the American. Frau Muller snorted her disgust.

She grabbed the American. His body was toned by regular gym and baseball practice. He lay hard against her. He did not fit her curves. She kissed him and tasted waffles and Moma's Pie.

'No fit,' she said.

She then grabbed the Italian. He was short—five inches shorter than Frau Muller. His pelvis did not meet her crotch. When they kissed, she could taste Chianti and garlic.

'No match,' she said.

The Frenchman took the imitative and grasped Frau Muller. He squeezed her breasts and forced his mouth upon her. He smelt of cheese and Sauterne.

'No match!' she shouted, affronted.

Lord March stepped forward. His large stomach fitted into Frau Muller's corseted stomach. Her breasts dropped graciously on his chest. The kiss was sweet, cream teas and English Gardens.

'Match!' she shouted, and led Lord March to her bedroom. 'Rate fixing, bah!'

# MUJI SLIPPERS

I received an invitation to spend the weekend at Lady Turnbull's London home, at the same time as George received a similar invitation. George rang me up and proudly said he had been invited, but his response withered like a punctured balloon when I said, 'Likewise me.' I received the invitation because I was made Lady Entrepreneur of London, and Lady Turnbull is a Conservative alderman, but often I am known in the circles in which George and Lady Turnbull move as 'Miss Toilet' because I organize contract cleaning.

George is, of course, in love with me, although he is not yet conscious of his feelings. He lives on a private income, and comes from an old English land-owning family, squeaky clean.

To return to the invitation, there was a Mayfair address on the embossed card, a time for arrival (cocktail hour) and then underneath in bold letters:

**PRISTINE FLOORING—NO OUTSIDE SHOES, NO STILETTO HEELS.**

*Oh dear,* I thought. I have encountered this kind of invitation before. There is a marked increase in the number of people who have 'pristine flooring' and take pains to prevent guests marking it with dirt or unsuitable shoes. They expect the guests to remove their shoes on arrival and put on some of those awful muji slippers which the hostess supplies. Meanwhile, the butler whisks away your outside shoes which are returned outside your bedroom door.

I had hoped this weekend would be an occasion on which I could impress George with my looks and taste. I had been shopping. I took my new Christian Dior clothes out of the wardrobe, swirling red skirt and pink top, which went so well with my high-heeled Bennett shoes. These were the clothes I had hoped to arrive in. Then I picked out a Vibe sheath in lace black evening wear, and laid beside them the new Russell and Bromley shoes.

If I did not wear the high-heeled shoes with my outfits, I would look like a mad gnome. I am only just five feet and not quite slim. I could not wear the muji slippers. I would be a laughing stock, even more than in the 'Miss Toilet' jibe. George would not fall in love with me.

So I decided to go in muji slippers and change into high heels at the door and later give the muji slippers to the maid.

I braved the path up to Lady Turnbull's mansion in the paper slippers, then gave the muddy muji slippers to the astounded maid. I put on my four-inch high-heeled Bennett shoes and moved across the large area room, converted so that two walls were now a huge window. I hoped that the whole of London would see me in my Christian Dior outfit.

George was there with drink in hand and an air of hazy desires. He wore muji slippers and looked fat, bald, and ravishing. I got him to tell me the directions to his bedroom which he was most reluctant to reveal.

As we were talking so cosily, Lord Turnbull approached.

'Oh the lady contract cleaner,' he said. 'How interesting, Florence Nightingale went to Germany to study drains. Did you know . . .' he droned on.

Lady Turnbull finally decided to intervene. 'Miss Elliot', she said, looking at my Bennett high-heeled shoes, 'the maid has not given you any slippers. How remiss.'

I said, 'I left them at the front door.'

'How strange,' she replied. 'I'll call the butler,' and she used her mobile phone.

The butler soon appeared. I had to put on the muji slippers. I looked in the window. My reflection was there for all London to see–dumpy, short, and overdressed.

I decided to go to bed, ambiguously saying to George, 'See you later.'

My bedroom was beside the drain. I had been put in one of the maids' rooms. The gurgling was a curse; the bed was narrow and hard. I took off my clothes and the muji slippers, and left them outside hoping the maid would throw them away. I wanted to wear my glitter heels tomorrow.

I had no en suite in my maid's room, and I wanted to go to the toilet in the night. So I went downstairs passed George's room, and saw he had left out the dirty shoes he came in for the maid.

In the morning, I sneaked downstairs again and saw the maid had taken the shoes from outside George's door. She had left muji slippers outside mine. I threw these away in the bin. My Bennett shoes had not been returned by the butler, so I decided to put on my glitter Russell and Bromley shoes.

I met George who was sitting on a sofa in the lounge, reading a newspaper.

'Why are you wearing evening shoes?' he said. He had on muji slippers.

'The slippers are so much more seductive. We could romp,' and he put his feet on my lap.

Later in the day, the Butler announced, 'For the sake of hygiene, all guests will be issued with new muji slippers.'

However, there were none outside my room. I went to the floor below. Fresh muji slippers were outside George's room, and also I was surprised to see outside Lady Turnbull's. (It was rumoured she no longer slept with Lord Turnbull.)

At the long formal dinner, I was placed beside Alderman Flint. His conversation was loud and obnoxious, about public lavatories in the city. His intent was to demean me.

When I could extricate myself from the company, I stood in my glitter shoes and evening dress in front of the glass window. Chic and expensive, no one could call me 'Miss Toilet'.

The lack of en suite meant that I had to go down to George's floor about an hour after retiring. I could see a male figure wearing muji slippers going towards Lady Turnbull's room.

Surely it couldn't be! Yes, it was George, short and bald. Lady Turnbull's slippers had been taken in. Primark walking boots had been left outside Lady Turnbull's door. George knocked, and she came out in muji slippers. Tall, elegant, and with long legs—she looked fabulous.

George, I now noticed, also carried walking boots.

Hand in hand, George and Lady Turnbull went down the corridor in their muji slippers, holding their getaway boots in their hands.

And I was left high and dry in my Russell and Bromley glitter shoes.

# PET-SHOP BOY

'Louisa and Gabrielle were taking coffee in Louisa's drawing room. Both were glamorous, both were in their thirties, neither was married. Louisa, the blonde, wore a silk jumpsuit, and Gabrielle, the brunette wore a lacy shirt and skirt. On the wall hung an original Constable and on the floor, a Peking rug. Both items were legacies from Louisa's husband, a dealer in Art and Fine Objects, now dead. Gabrielle's husband was alive, a politician and errant husband.'

Gabrielle and Louisa reverted to a subject which had intrigued them for two years, concerning a neighbour in their gated community who had refused all their kind invitations for drinks or dinner. If he had been old or ugly or if he had had a wife, this would merely have been construed as a breach of manners, but he was young and handsome and seemingly single. Louisa and Gabrielle frequently spoke of his refusals wistfully in their conversations. They longed to meet him.

He had joined the Resident's Association and had given Colonel Rutherford his subscription willingly enough, but he would not attend any meetings or events. Louisa and Gabrielle were determined to smoke him out.

The Hungarian maid came in with the sherry tray. Gabrielle took a glass and mused.

'I know a girl friend of mine who was anxious to make a neighbour her friend. She "accidentally" ran into the wing mirror of his car with her car. She knew wing mirrors can be easily adjusted, but she pretended she had committed an awful offense and she knocked on his door, contrite and upset, full of tearful apologises. He knew it was only a minor problem, but he was moved by her tears, asked her in for a drink, then out to dinner. She e-mailed me last week that they were engaged.'

Louisa said, 'I don't want to risk damaging his car, but you have given me food for thought.'

Gabrielle disappeared for a lunch date, leaving Louisa to spin her web.

Louisa peeked into the Family Room. A much-loved cat lay with her kittens in a velvet-covered basket. She thought, *The kittens will be walking around and out of the basket in a couple of weeks. Their mum, Angelica, will be free for a bit of spying.*

Unlike a lot of residents in the gated community, the good-looking bachelor did his own gardening. Passers-by had seen him planting and tending to his bulbs. They called over to him, he waved back, friendly enough, but he never invited conversation.

Angelica had never been microchipped. Her name and address were on a pasted paper at the back of the collar. Louisa had removed the telephone number for this morning. She wanted the good-looking bachelor to call at her house, not just briefly telephone.

She took Angelica in her arms and, checking that no one was looking, she placed her cat in the good-looking man's garden amongst the sprouting bulbs.

'*Dig, Angelic, dig,*' she willed the cat. *He will think you wandered down the road on your own. He will pick you up, see whose cat you are, and return you to me. I will cry, tell* you you are a naughty girl, and throw myself into his arms in remorse. Then after he has agreed to a reconciliation dinner, I will give you a lovely fresh haddock and cream.

But this isn't quite what happened. The good-looking man had seen Louisa and Angelica on the drive. His shyness had all disappeared. He became loving and expansive. He came up to Angelica and Louisa and stroked the cat. He took it from Louisa and held it to him.

'Oh, you beauty, come into my house and have some milk.'

He brought her into his house and Louisa followed.

'Oh, she's wonderful,' said the good-looking man. 'I have always wanted a cat like her. What's her name?'

'Angelica,' said Louisa. 'Can I introduce her to you, by your Christian name? We only know you as Mr Barnes on the Estate. Too formal for a feline friend.'

'Simon, I'm Simon Barnes,' he said.

So now at last she knew. *Simon* . . . how nice.

'I'm Louisa,' she said.

'I know, I asked,' he said as he looked in her eyes and continued to fondle Angelica.

'Angelica had four kittens last month. They look like her. If you want to see them, come to my house.'

'Now, oh yes, I would love to.'

They walked through the wooded cul-de-sac to Louise's house, which was set apart near the woodland at the entry to the gated community.

The decoy had worked. Angelica and Louisa had snared the good-looking bachelor.

Louise took Simon into the Family Room. The kittens were roaming around. Simon put Angelica down, and picked up a kitten which strongly resembled the mother.

'Is it a girl?' said Simon.

'Yes,' said Louisa. 'She will be ready to go to a new home in two weeks.'

'She'll be mine. She'll be called Louisa after you,' said Simon, adding shyly, 'If you don't mind.'

'No, how lovely. How did you know my name?'

'I've asked about you. I have seen you walking about the Estate. You are so gorgeous. I have fallen in love with you.'

'Well, why didn't you speak to me? Or come to my parties when I put a card through your door?'

'I didn't fancy those parties where you stand around with a drink in your hand, making small talk. I wanted you. You and your friends all seemed so important and superior, I guess I was shy—frightened of making a fool of myself.'

'But we were all wanting to get to know you. Good-looking bachelors are a rarity here.'

'Well, Louisa, you must know I am only a chap who runs a chain of pet shops. I'm not an artist or a distinguished author.

'My Pet Shop boy,' said Louise taking his hand.

'My two Louisas,' said Simon, holding the kitten and Louise in a loving threesome.

# TAKING THE PISS

The station was clean, the pale-green woodwork freshly painted. I looked around. No cans or fish and chip papers thrown into the corners. No 'deprived' young people smoking fags. Flower baskets hung over the sign 'WELCOME TO BUCKLAND AND ROEHAMPTON'. To myself, I added, *Welcome to Dominic Liddle, your Tory candidate.*

Sir Peter Ogilvie had come to meet me himself, accompanied by his wife. He was dressed in tweeds and a cap, in contrast to the formal suit I had seen him in before at the Selection Committee. His wife, Beatrice, was by his side, smiling and waving at me. She was thin, wearing a steel-grey suit, and there was a severe birdlike look in her eye.

They took me in their old Bentley to Towers Place, where I was to stay the night after the Adoption Meeting. Towers Place did indeed have two three-story towers, book-ending the long two-storey building. The frontage looked neglected and a little crumbling. I blamed the successive Labour Governments who had bled the flower of our gentry of their rightful inheritance. The sitting room I was taken into had taste, yet it was shabby. Beatrice's angry eyes roved round the room settling on the fading fabric, denied succour by public theft.

'We've put you in the Tower, Dominic,' said Sir Peter. 'There's a fine view of the grounds, and a bedroom, sitting room, desk, and computer. There's no private bathroom, I'm afraid. The possibility was drained away by taxes.'

'We have to keep all these unmarried mothers now, you know,' Beatrice said. 'When I was young, they would have been sent to reformatories to scrub floors. Naughty girls!' and she wagged her finger, like a matron in my school.

We went back down the stairs, and they showed me the bathroom and toilet I was to use. It was two flights down from the Tower, by the Ogilvies' bedroom.

We had dinner in the dining room, a sparse trio round the huge table. The dinner was a sardine salad followed by a shop trifle. We spoke of my old public school, which their son had also attended, and speculated on which members of the Shadow Cabinet would hold ministerial posts when the Conservative Government was re-elected.

'Not you this time, you'll be a new Member, Dominic. But maybe you will be in the Government in the next Parliament, if you make the right impression.'

Sir Peter and I drove to the Conservative Club, for my Adoption Meeting, followed by a drinks party.

'You'll do fine,' the Chairman said. 'I'm sure we'll be proud of you. You'll make us pleased to have you as our MP, judging by your curriculum vitae. Nothing out of the way. Nothing potty about you, like some of these chaps. You know campaigning for Gay Adoption or whatnot.'

It was drinks all round. Everyone toasted me. I was the rising star. I was on the ladder towards the top.

Beatrice had retired to bed when we got back. I said 'goodnight' to Peter, and crept up the two flights of stairs to my bedroom. My feelings of euphoria wore off when I realized I had not been to the lavatory. I might wake Beatrice if I went downstairs. She might come out of her room, stern, in a robe. I decided to remove my suit and put on my dressing gown. I got the suit off and hung it in the cupboard, and, as if by magic, a chamber pot fell out. It was the most beautiful and desirable thing I had ever seen. It was large, with a blue Wedgwood design. I had never had a more welcome present. My spirits rose. I need not go to the bathroom; I could use the pot and empty it in the morning before the Ogilvies got up.

The evening's beer made its demands and I pissed lustily into the pot for this reason waking three times in the night.

Heavy of head, I did not wake at my alarm clock's bidding, silencing it with my sleepy hand at 7.30 a.m. The smells of breakfast woke me an hour later. I could hear the Ogilvies moving about, his shuffling gait and her scolding voice.

They were in the corridor between their bedroom and the dining room. I looked at the nauseous brown swirl in the pot, fuming like a polluted tropical lagoon. I could not face Beatrice bearing this. My filth in her family heirloom.

I heard the Matron's voice, 'Naughty boy, what have you done now, you will have to explain to the Headmaster.'

I became a quaking schoolboy again.

Perhaps if I waited ten minutes while they were in the dining room having breakfast, I could sneak down with the pot and pour the content into the toilet. I advanced with the pot down the first flight of stairs. With the ears of a greyhound, Beatrice had heard me.

'Dominic' she said 'What are you dithering about for up there? I am serving breakfast.

'Coming,' I said. I could not move with the pot, which was now shaking in my hand, its contents about to sully the carpet, so I retreated to my bedroom, placed the pot in a corner and went down to the dining room without it.

At breakfast, the Ogilvies noticed my anxiety and loomed over me at the table with disapproval. Did I really have it in me for the fight in the constituency? The agent had phoned to say that urgent business had cropped up that morning, and that he would take me on the planned tour of the Constituency in the afternoon. The Ogilvies had said earlier that they planned to stay in that morning.

To pursue the vexed problem of the pot, I told Beatrice I had e-mails to send, and I returned upstairs. The pot sat accusingly by my bed, and the smell had gained in venom. I was becoming desperate, even little deranged. The Tower rooms faced to the back, unlike the Ogilvie's rooms which fronted the sweeping lawns and drives at the front. I looked out at the back garden and noticed for the first time a greenhouse at the side of the house. The door was swinging open. Surely that was the natural home for a pot, and human waste the natural fertilizer for a garden.

My plan solidified. If I could get out of the sitting-room window, by the balustrade above the second floor, I could carry the pot, and then walk it by stages on the window ledges, while I climbed down the pipe at the near end of the other tower and the main building. Then I could jump down into the garden, throw the urine on the flower beds and put the pot in the greenhouse, with the other pots.

I took my first tentative steps and got out of the window and carried the pot along the balustrade. The pot wobbled, some of the piss fell out, but I presumed the odour would be carried away by the wind. When I got to the pipe I was in deep trouble. I could not balance. The pot fell to the garden with a crash. My foot was caught. There was a loud noise. The alarm had gone off. Peter and Beatrice had rushed to the back garden, followed by several passers-by. Beatrice picked up one of the pieces of the pot. Her face was a mask of horror and contempt. A crowd gathered. The police arrived. I was still tangled with the pipe.

Someone shouted, 'It's that Tory candidate. Is this a stunt for *Fathers 4 Justice*?'

The Fire Brigade came and rescued me from the pipe. My trousers were torn in the most embarrassing place. Girls were jeering and pointing.

Beatrice said, 'There is no excuse for this sort of behaviour. Send him home. Naughty boy.'

After the paramedics had ensured I had no injury, I was put on the next train to London. Peter and Beatrice did not drive me to the station.

The Police, Central Office, and Fleet Street had all separately put together the story of what had happened. I lay in my bed in my Park Lane flat. The newspapers started to come through my door, sent by the usual 'well-wishers'.

I read the headlines:

'We . . . We . . . We . . . Will Overcome. Liddle Piddle . . . Taking the Piss.'

'Potty' followed by a picture of a large pot, with the Tory Shadow Cabinet in it.

And so on. I got up, telephoned the Chairman, resigned as candidate and fled abroad.

# PERFORMANCE

## SOUL SEARCHING

2 Angels –Rafael and Stephen – 2 male actors
Lucifer – man or woman

Action takes place on Earth

*Stephen enters with a big sack full of souls of the recently dead.*

**Rafael** More souls? Bah.

**Stephen** Aren't we sorting out the souls anymore? The Good from the Bad?

**Rafael** Nah, we are just going to dump them in a black hole

**Stephen**

(Scandalized) what they did on earth didn't matter? Whether they made an Act of Contrition? Confession, Extreme Unction? Whether they were adulterers, liars, murderers?

**Rafael Nah**, there are too many of them. We would have to be here ages. *He* does not allow overtime, "They laboured in the vineyard day and night..." or so *He* says.

**Stephen** But this is eternal life you are denying some of them....just pushed in a black hole, what about Jesus and his Disciples, Holy Martyrs who suffered the agonies of Hell for our cause.

**Rafael** Look Stephen, the Gig is full. *He* doesn't allow touts. The Martyrs go in the black hole same as the others. There is no room in the Inn, no affordable housing, nothing. They all gotta go down the black hole, whoever they are, whatever they did.

Stephen Hawkins will see they go to a parallel universe, where there may be more room. So shove 'em all down the black hole and we can go back to Heaven in time for the manna and mead.

**Stephen** We can't just go back without doing the job. *He* will know. Let's just open the bag and have a look at some of the souls.

*Pulls out a skull, with a face still visible. The soul is attached to the skull with sticky tape.*

I know who that is; he was that Dictator in Iraq, who killed so many people with genocide in the1980s and 90s. He should go to Hell.

**Rafael** Modern psychology would say he was a victim of circumstances, an orphan, who was forced to be a street fighter by his Uncle.

Tony Blaire and George Bush started the war not Sadam Hussein.

Anyway he was a Muslim, We are Christian angels, and we read the Bible not the Koran.

**Stephen** Then why is his soul in our bag?

**Rafael** Incompetence of American angels.

Chuck it back in the bag, and when Lucifer comes, he will draw the evil souls to him and take them back to Hell

**Stephen** So Lucifer has his pick of souls, before God can make any judgement or show any mercy?

**Rafael** In Hell there are now many scientific developments, which God's Council have judged unlawful. Lucifer can see with X ray eyes, and can spot an evil soul without any resource to interrogation or perusal of records. He draws them to him like a magnet, and carries them off to Hell.

Look up. He flies above us now. He is drawn to the soul bag.

**Stephen.** He will take Saddam Hussein.

**Rafael** Perhaps. Let us hide behind these trees, or he might take us. Leave the soul bag on the ground.

**Lucifer**

*Comes onto the stage, dressed in a suit of black, and a red and gold crown, to advertise the wealth of Hell. He picks up the soul bag, and stirs it with his hand,*

L Bah! I seek pure evil. This is liberal twaddle and relativism! An evil spirit would fly to me as kindred. I must rummage in the bag.

*He pulled out a skull.* Saddam Hussein said to be a mass murderer. Political. Like those tried at the Hague Convention. I do not deal in such ifs and buts. Let me throw Saddam Hussein's soul back in the pile.

But haste me there is another soul of pure evil exciting my X ray eyes, I will draw it out. Its designation reads

**Christopher Hamilton Smith**-a former Bank Manager, at the Clydesdale Bank in Aberdeen. A truly evil man.

**Stephen.** We know that man. He was always spoken of as fair dealing. A family man, kept his garden well, the outside of his house painted every five years and the inside, three, washed his clothes with Ariel.

**Rafael** See how his soul cleaves to the Devil! He is the Devil's own.

*Lucifer minces his way off stage, caressing the soul of Christopher Hamilton Smith. He turns to the audience and gives a wicked grin and a rude sign.*

*Lucifer gives the Soul of Christopher to his Second in Command, Beelzebub (off stage) and returns. Rafael and Stephen remain behind the Trees.*

**Lucifer** I want a female soul, beautiful and wanton, that I can call my own. Ah here this is the one **Sin**, she will be my wife and companion, who will bear my son **Death**. She will stand to outshine Mary in Heaven, to eclipse her insipid goodness with our Evil.

**Rafael** *(from behind the tree)* That young woman, is Cynthia Jones, she died in a house fire, which her mentally ill brother started. She was ordinary – a typist – no criminal record.

**Stephen** And now she is Queen of Hell. There is little sense in this proceeding.

**Lucifer** bah

# THE SIGNING

The shelves of books rose high around him, daring the cultural mountaineers to climb their peaks. On the narrow piece of flooring in the dark valley beneath them, Simon's chair and desk entombed him. He had been signing books for over an hour, and his performance had become like monk in a cell writing a repetitive prayer.

'How many more?' he said to the shop assistant.

'Well, sir', he said, respectfully, 'they are queueing down the stairs and outside as far as Boots.'

'Two deep?' asked Simon

'Three deep,' said the assistant. 'There are going to be bumper sales.'

'Well, let's go on then,' said Simon.

*'To Jane with love, To Tommy from Sarah,' and so I sign on as the customer wishes*, said Simon to himself. His head felt heavy, and he was dragged down by an unaccountable grief.

A slim and somehow familiar hand, proffered a copy of *Horror Lives*, a whisper said, 'Please write *To Flora Xmark, my true heart, from Simon James.*'

Like a zombie, Simon wrote as he was bid. He hardly saw the woman from his confined chair, and she quickly bolted through the crowd, but the name hammered on his brain, Flora Xmark.

'Flora, Flora!' he shouted, 'Come back, what did I write, *my own heart*, come back!'

Someone in the queue jumped up and down with excitement, maybe this was a celebrity event, which would make it the magazines. Simon rose as if to force his way through the queue. The shop assistant put a restraining hand on him.

'The customers, sir. They have all brought *Horror Lives*. You must sign their copies now.'

Simon was trapped. His mouth was dry, he could hardly breathe, but he continued signing until there was no more need. His hands were clammy; he felt hot. He ran out of the shop and down the main shopping street, waylaying people.

'Have you seen Flora Xmark? Tall and slim?'

'You a nut? Lost your woman, have you—ha ha' and other comments.

Then one said, 'You that writer chap? Is this a stunt? Will we soon see the gore?'

A crowd gathered, a policeman appeared.

Simon said, 'Have you seen Flora Xmark?'

'Child? Missing person?' asked the policeman.

'A ghost,' said Simon.

'Oh you're that writer chap. We don't have ghosts here. Don't block the pathway.'

Through his distracted mental haze, Simon eventually found his car in the car park. He snail led with the traffic to Queen's Road, where he was sharing a rented flat with his research assistant, Bob. Bob was not in, so Simon collapsed on a chair while he pondered on the message he had written in Flora Xmart's copy of *Horror Lives*. He had said she was 'my own true heart' after her thirty-second reappearance in his life. The key turned in the lock, and Bob, a burley 22-year-old, came into the room. He knew Flora had been part of Simon's life in the years he wrote twenty successful romances, and thought the signing of 'my own heart' would definitely appeal to what he believed to be her mercenary spirit. Simon agreed; after all, she had sequestered the flat they had shared and all its valuable contents.

'I can see her now on "Breakfast TV" saying she is my heart, the repository of all my secrets on a tell-all programme.'

'What are these secrets?' said Bob, with a grin 'Are they very horrible?'

'No one ever knows another's horror,' said Simon 'No, you find out where she is, and get the book back. It's her evidence. Report back to me.'

Bob easily traced Flora Xmark. In fact, she was living in a flat not far from theirs. First, he pretended to be a window cleaner and looked in the flat. There were piles of romances by Simon, but he could not see *Horror Lives* or any other of the horror stories Simon had written after he gave up romances.

He decided a more direct approach that might appeal to her vanity and sent her a letter saying he was writing a book about contemporary romantic writing, adding that she was thought to be the muse of Simon James. Could he meet her and take photographs?

He followed this letter up with a phone call, and she hesitatingly gave him an appointment. When he told Simon of these developments, Simon said Bob's mission was finished, he would confront her himself.

Simon went to the expensive apartment block where Bob said Flora lived. He realised he had once shared her life there.

Simon pressed the bell with Flora's flat number. He was surprised that the bell tolled like a crier in the Middle Ages, the theme of *Bring Out Your Dead*. Flora's hesitant voice could be heard guiding him to the fourth floor. Dying plants flanked the door, and then her face was revealed, still lovely but pale and contorted.

'Simon, alone?' she said, but not surprised. Perhaps she had always seen through the 'Bob' ruse. 'Come in,' she said in the same expressionless voice.

The living room she led him into was bright and modern as he remembered it, but the pictures on the walls jarred— childlike coloured prints and dark oils. At her request, he sat in a cushioned chair, but its comfortable appearance belied its miss-fit for the human form. There was a smell in the room of vegetable decay; and when he touched the coffee table, it seemed to cringe. His book, *Horror Lives*, resting on the coffee table, seemed to move from his hand. He forced the seemingly reluctant book back to his grasp. The author opened his work and looked at the fly leaf. The writing said,

*To my own heart, yours to Flora.*

Is that what he had really written? The writing had not been altered. Had the book itself altered the inscription? He put it down hurriedly.

He looked at Flora's distorted face and saw her eyes were full of pain. He had expected triumph. She put a restraining hand on his as it moved to *Horror Lives* again.

Then out of the fog of his mind, he seemed to remember living in this flat with Flora, but his memory was like a chaotic dream, dark and light. He remembered sleepless nights when he could not think or write, when the bedroom walls seemed to narrow, and he felt he could not fight them off, images later transposed into the black, sticky tunnel in which the hero of *Horror Lives* was trapped. The numb zombie who guarded his head, was like the guards in *Horror Lives*. Like the hero of his book, he had felt trapped in a chair, by invisible bonds, unable to move. Hate stared at him like a dog at bay. He could no longer respond to love. His vision blurred out all affection; his slow movements killed desire.

Then Flora knelt in front of him.

'When we broke up, we both fell into a depression, your books mirror that. I find them painful to read. We were part of each other; we should never have split over that trivial thing—Jane.'

The green left her face, and her features became soft and translucent. The room seemed beautifully proportioned again, and Simon's hands felt no longer clammy, nor his body unable to rise from the chair. Indeed he rose and embraced Flora.

'My own true heart, there has never been another, only the black pit of loneliness, the feeling of separation and depression.'

Simon started to write romances again. The reviewers commented on their truth and depth of feeling.

# ARCHIE LEARNS THE MODERN WAY

The landlord came into Archie's room without knocking. Ted was helping Archie into his trousers.

The landlord was called Mr Maurice. He brought the news that they would temporarily have to leave the house because of structural repairs needed on the property.

In order to foreshorten Ted's wail and Archie's anger, Mr Maurice said, 'I will send the Council Housing officer to see you. They know I am a good social landlord.'

'But the rent . . .,' Ted started to say, but Mr Maurice had gone.

'Council Housing,' said Archie. 'Unmarried mothers, druggies, ne'r do wells who don't work. I held rank in the army, you know.'

'Until you were asked to fight and went AWOL.'

The phone rang. They were told that the Housing Department would see them the next day.

At Housing, they were asked to sign a form verifying their names, ages, etc.

They were told to go into a room where a plain, bespectacled woman said one word. 'Needs?'

Archie looked cheery, 'All the usual and extras.'

The Housing officer took off her glasses, which made her look much more appealing.

'I shall report you, you naughty boy. Income?' she said, looking doubtfully at Ted.

'I have an army pension,' said Archie, 'Officer class. Ted here was my batman.'

'DSS' the form is easier for us to fill in. You will be a claimant, no rent to pay.'

The Housing officer summoned another woman. They conferred. Archie could hear 'sexual harassment'.

The other woman—a fat, unpleasant party—said to Archie and Ted, 'You must go to the Integration Course at Bedford Road Community Centre as a condition of your tenancy. You have already shown a disregard for Equal Opportunities.'

An old woman collected Archie and Ted from the foyer of the block they were to live in. She guided them to the Common Room. A dark-skinned woman in a kaftan opened the door. She pulled Archie and Ted through the door, and then slammed it in the old woman's face. 'Integration?'

Archie and Ted stood by the door. When Ted tried to sit in one of the empty seats, angry voices pushed him back. Archie remained aloof.

An angry official said to them, 'You must integrate, or you cannot have a DSS flat.'

Then a Conservative Woman councillor, in whose ward was the enclave of council housing, got up to speak, her voice toned by finishing school.

'Now everyone of British origin is to hand a cup of tea to one of our new immigrants.'

One man threw the tea in a Pole's face. He started shouting. Archie, followed by Ted, moved forward, bent double as if stalking in a jungle. They handed the tea to the fat woman in the kaftans, everybody laughed.

The community worker said, 'Now you have integrated with Maria, you must take her out for dinner next week, when you have the DSS cheque.'

She continued, 'You must be a gentleman and not sexually exploit her.'

Archie looked at Ted, amazed. 'Her?' he whispered.

'You made a sexist joke to the Housing officer when she asked you about Needs.'

'If an officer is female, you can only compliment her on her work skills and qualifications. For instance to me you would say, "I have never seen a community worker handle an Integration Meeting better. You must have a PhD from Poland."'

Then Mr Maurice the landlord came in to bare the Conservative councillor away.

'Will the repairs be completed by next week?' shouted the frantic Ted, after him.

# BACON SANDWICH

'Caroline, my sister, has asked us to go to this charity event. I suppose the guests will be pretty poor because she says "outfits" are provided. The charity had some initials, like I saw outside Greg's, so the guests maybe are the starving too.'

'Do we have to go to meet all these poor, naked people?' said Ted.

'Yes,' Archie said. 'We must keep in with Caroline. I owe her a lot of money. You must come with me, batman.'

'I'll go in an evening dress to distinguish myself from the naked poor, and you go in that boiler suit, which made such a hit at the Conservative Garden Party which Boris Johnson attended. That will please Caroline.'

'Anyway if we have to go naked, we will have the sandwich advertisement board, to cover our fronts,' said Ted, hopefully.

'Maybe,' said Archie.

They went to City Hall in a taxi for which Caroline had paid in advance.

They were ushered into a room with a notice —

*Men Becoming Women.*

Archie frowned. In most papers it's —

*Men Seeking Women.*

The room was filled with dresses and skirts of all sizes, and underwear copied from the Moulin Rouge.

On the wall was written - **GLBTS.**

'The sandwiches with bacon and tomato from Greg's,' Archie said. 'They are the sponsors.'

Archie had not taken off his dinner jacket. A slim, dark-haired lady approached him; the whore's face was very made up. To Archie, she looked like a prostitute.

'How much are the sandwiches?' he said, winking gamely.

'Oh, we don't do that here', she said, 'it's one on one.'

Archie did not know what to say. His beautiful partner led him on to the dance floor.

Archie tried to dance. A man pushed in with shorts and braces.

'Fred's my boyfriend,' he said. Archie's date took off his shirt and bra.

He looked for Ted to ask him if he knew what was going on.

He was thwarted when he saw Ted in his boiler suit, with SLAVE written on the back in felt-tip pen. He was dancing with a tall, blond willowy man, who was asking him about his wages. Then Archie realised, this was his sister Caroline, in drag. She was trying to get Ted away from him with talk of wages.

Archie grabbed Ted and hauled him off.

'We're going to Gregg's for a BLT Trans sexual sandwich.'

# YOU'VE GOTTA HAVE
# SOMETHING IN THE BANK

Ted called to see Archie. He found him squeezing himself into a suit.

'Jack Mullins has written,' said a breathless Archie. 'He sent me an appointment for 9.30 a.m. Does't he realize I have my breakfast then? I nearly phoned to make it ten o'clock, but it's probably easier to go when the creep suggests.'

'He's the manager at the Bank now, isn't he? Is he suggesting you bring him flowers to mark his promotion?' said Ted.

'Of course not. I am a dissatisfied customer. I am going as a complainant,' said Archie.

'What are you complaining about, Archie?' asked Ted, perching himself on the end of the cluttered table.

'His machines don't work. I've tried five in the last two days. No money came out of them even when I hit them with my stick. Then when I shouted at them, they spat my card back at me. I shall tell Mullins of this discourtesy.'

'You went to school with Mullins, didn't you?' said Ted.

'He was a creep,' said Archie. 'He was the only boy whose stink bomb didn't go off in the lab on April 1. He came out smelling of roses and was made a prefect. He won't get away with it this time. Not when I've made my complaint.'

'Let's see that letter, Archie.'

'He talks about a draft, overdraft,' said Archie 'Trying to get out of it. I was in no draught. His machines are faulty. They always have some excuse. I remember when I complained about that pie—'

Ted interrupted him,

'The letter says you owe the Bank money. You have taken out more than you have put in.'

'How could I have taken out more money if the machines don't work?' said Archie, his face now red.

'The letter says you have got to see Jack Mullins to authorize a loan,' said Ted.

'But I don't want a loan!' shouted Archie 'I want the machines to work so that I can get my money out.'

'They say if you don't pay the loan back, you could become bankrupt, and they will,'—Ted paused—'se-ques-ter your possessions.' He looked round the room doubtfully.

'Those bottles?' said Archie, eyeing the small army of empties.

'Spent liquidity,' said Ted.

'He can replace them as well as his machines,' said Archie, forcing his arms into his overcoat and grabbing his stick to go into battle.

# BOO BOO

Caroline telephoned her brother Archie. She said, 'Darling, would you be a marvel and have Boo Boo for a few days?'

'Who is she? Where will she sleep, here?'

'Oh, on your knee or in bed with you?'

*What?* thought Archie. *Who did she say? Which one is Boo Boo?*

'I'll bring her at 4 p.m. today, and collect her on Friday. I'll phone you on Friday morning. Love and kisses, from little sister.'

Panic stricken, Archie knocked on Ted's door.

'Boo Boo's coming,' said Archie.

'Coming?' said Ted, 'The knockout pole dancer?' he said and collapsed by the door. 'Is she bringing a pole? Where is she going to sleep?'

'In my bed or on my knee,' said Archie, a smile now crossing his cheek.

'We've got no pole in here?' said Ted, who had not yet digested Archie's last answer.

'There is a pole in the garden that Mrs Philips uses for hanging out the washing. Bring it up here like a good fellow, while I dress.'

Archie put on his most expensive casual wear, white chinos and a navy sweater with a nautical motif. He could not do enough to impress Boo Boo.

He began to fantasise. *Would she be a tall blonde who would dance seductively round the pole? Or a little darling jenny wren who would wear French knickers?*

Ted reappeared with the washing-line pole.

'It's wet,' said Archie. 'Dry it, Ted. If she wants it wet, she will say so.'

The afternoon wore on. Archie walked up and down secretly scared his sexual performance would not match up to the pole dancer's experience.

At 4 p.m., these worries were dissolved. Caroline, expensively yet formally dressed, was at Archie's door holding a cat basket and a carrier bag from which a cat litter tray and a packet of litter could be seen.

Caroline opened the cat-basket door.

'Come on, Boo Boo, meet your uncle Archie. You two are going to have real fun together. Oh, you have already got a scratch pole in the flat. How thoughtful of you, Archie.'

Boo Boo came out of her basket. She was a beautiful seal point Siamese. Long, undulating in her walk, beautiful blue eyes, and when she meowed at Archie, there was a yearning, a definite yearning.

When Caroline had left for her mini Conservative Conference. Boo Boo took one tender look at Archie. She climbed the pole, which was just behind Archie's chair.

Ted could see her weaving her way up, her tits showing as she moved from side to side. At the top of the pole she seemed to wave, and then she jumped down neatly into Archie's lap.

# DESIRABLE

'Both of you? Well, fine, come in,' said Dr Marat, emerging from behind his newspaper. 'Sit down. What can I do for you?'

'My hearing is too good,' said Archie. 'Could I have an ear operation, so that the TV sounds normal?'

'Have you tried turning it down?' asked the doctor. 'Most men of your age would be glad to hear so well. How old are you two now?' He looked in the computer.

'Archibald Hamilton Smyth, 64, and Edward Jones, 60. When did you two last have a medical? When you left the army, fifteen years ago, it says here,' said Dr Marat, looking in the computer again.

'Well, I will weigh and measure Archie first. On the scales, 120 kilos—too much—and your height?' he said, bringing the measure to Archie's standing figure, 5'9", two inches less than when you left the Army. You weigh much more than the desirable weight for a man of your height.'

'So I am no longer desirable?' said an annoyed Archie, 'Mandy doesn't think so. Genevieve at the Club doesn't think so. Weigh Ted, see if he's a desirable weight.'

Ted stood on the scales.

'He measures in at a svelte 80 kilos. He is still 5'9" as he had been in the army,' Archie fumed. 'I had to lead men. That's what made my shoes wear down. Ted just followed me.'

He added another punch. 'That scrawny, ill-bred creature is not more desirable than me.'

There were noises and a scuffle outside the door; a woman was shouting.

Archie didn't hear, Ted said, 'What's that?'

'What's what?' said Archie.

'That's the horrid laugh of a woman brandishing a knife. She wants to kill me, although I am of desirable weight,' said Dr Marat.

He continued, 'Now Archie, I will give you a diet sheet. No beer, for a start or only two pints a week. No chips or pies, you will see all that in there.'

'But I have got to live my life, see my friends, play billiards.'

'Well, you can do all those things, but no beer or whiskey.'

Ted intervened, 'We only came about Archie's hearing. We didn't come to hear we couldn't drink beer and that we were undesirable. Anyway, only birds are undesirable.'

There was a noise outside the door. Dr Marat looked resigned. Ted and Archie moved towards the door. A young woman with dark hair stood brandishing a knife. She moved the knife towards the doctor's throat, shouting 'undesirable!'

Archie and Ted slipped away, out of the Health Centre.

# IN THE BEGINNING

'I often talk to God, you know,' said Archie, a large red-faced man in his sixties.

'You mean like prayers in a church,' said Ted, his ferret-faced next-door neighbour.

'No, I talk to him in my bath, shout to him when I am over the TV, when I am in my chair,' said Archie. 'I say, "Well God let's have a chat."'

'Does he reply?' said Ted.

'Oh yes, I know what he says. He likes our chats,' said Archie.

''Av you asked him if he made the world in six days?' said Ted.

'Well, actually I have, and if he made day and night too.'

'Yes', said Ted, 'and all the animals and plants. At school we used to sing a hymn at Harvest Festivals, *All good gifts around us are sent from heaven above.* So did he send them all?'

'Yes, he sends them all, and day and night too, but not the evenings in the summer,' said Archie.

'How do you mean?' said Ted. 'What's so different about the evenings in the summer?'

'Well, I was talking to God, shouting over the television murder mystery, when I heard this loud voice saying that the summer evenings were brought by *Birds Eye Simply Fish.*'

'So he's contracted out the summer evenings to *Birds Eye Simply Fish*, because he's broke?' said Ted.

'Maybe he can't get the staff where He is,' said Archie.

'If the fish people are a subsidiary of God, maybe he will put them on the Board of Directors, then it would be *God the Father, Jesus the Son, the Holy Ghost, and Birds Eye Simply Fish* we would pray to,' said Ted.

'Could be,' said Archie. 'I'll ask him when I have our next chat.'

# A RUSSIAN MISSILE

Archie banged furiously on Ted's door at 9 a.m.

'Hey, squadie, quick march, enemy cited,' he shouted.

Ted came out, his breakfast eggs around his mouth.

'Aye, aye, Captain,' he said, brandishing his toast like a weapon. 'Where's the enemy?'

'There's the enemy,' shouted Archie, jabbing his window with his walking stick. 'The tube with an eye, from Russia.'

'Phone the Army HQ,' said Ted. 'Don't delay, the order will come soon from Moscow—*fire*. It's all set up. The eye is on us.'

Ted thought again, recollecting how they had been discharged from the army for cowardly disobedience: he following his commanding officer, Archie, as a deserter. So he said to Archie, 'We both deserted the Army, they might drag us back, court martial us, better phone the police,' said Ted.

'OK, squaddie. You always knew how to hide. I'll phone 101 or shall I get Caroline to phone? She's always hugging up to the Police at the Conservative Party Dance,' said Archie.

'No,' said Ted, getting nervous at the thought of Caroline, Archie's sister. 'You phone.'

'There is a missile pointing to my bedroom window,' said Archie to the duty sergeant who was based at the local Police Pod.

'Had a good night on the piss, did you?' said the Sergeant. 'OK, it's quite quiet here, so I can spare Constable Jones. He will be with you shortly to register the complaint.'

His parting words to the Constable were, 'If its wasting police time we can get them, have them both locked up, Archie and Ted they are called.'

Three quarters of an hour later, Constable Jones arrived at Archie and Ted's residence at 17 Arcadia Mews. They took him up to Archie's bedroom, gesticulating fiercely at 12 Arcadia Mews, opposite.

Constable Jones took one look at the supposed weapon.

'It's a telescopic lens,' he said. 'What do you do in here, Mr Hamilton Smyth? Entertain nude women, children in obscene poses?' And to himself he said, *Taking images of children would be much more serious charge than wasting police time. The Sergeant would be really pleased. Get the pair of them off the Manor.*

Then his phone rang, with an urgent call back to the Police Pod.

'Go call on your neighbours, you old rogues. Ask them what they are at with that telescopic eye. If you haven't planted it yourselves.'

As he went, Ted said, 'I am gasping, *Horse and Hounds*, Archie?'

'Lead the way, squad.'

When they entered the pub, they were greeted by raucous laughter and wolf whistles.

*Was it that woman I brought in here last week? We were pretty friendly,* he thought.

Then he saw the 60-inch curved TV the drinkers were crowded round. Someone familiar pushed him to the front.

The channel was *You Tube,* which he had never heard of before.

Then he realised the film was about him. His arse was shown struggling into his pants, his fat stomach quivered as he aimed his T-shirt at it. The next shot had him crawling along his bedroom floor, his little fat legs in the air. The film showed him washing his face, losing his soap then washing his face with a towel. Finally, he turned and took out a limp penis from his pants, fondled it as it grew.

The entire pub was laughing and whistling.

'It's you, Archie.'

Archie crawled out of the door.

'It will go viral,' said the Publican. 'It's that funny.'

'What's viral?' asked Ted.

'It will go all round the world!'

'To Russia?' asked Ted.

'Yes, to the Kremlin. Putin will laugh at it,' said the Publican.

# THE 'N' WORD

Ted burst into Archie's flat, terrified, as if he had to face a field of cows.

He said, 'The head librarian at the city's library has written to me. He said I used the "n" word in the Central Library. He says I must attend a course Reviewing My Vocabulary, at the behest of the Library Committee or be referred to a Commission.'

'Let me see that letter,' said Archie. 'Your reading standard is well below mine, that's why you were only my batman.'

'I never go to the library. I don't read books. I don't know what an "n" word is. I only got as far as "g" in my *Start Write* book. Tell them that.'

'You went to the library with me last week to carry out the volumes of *Contemporary Philosophy*. I was going to put them in my window to entice Jane to visit.'

'That long-legged University woman who passes our house every day? You've got the hots for her?'

Ignoring this question. Archie said, 'You said "nickers" to the librarian, that's what it is,' turning his whiskey glass sagely.

'I thought it was "knickers", with a "k", said the not-so-ignorant Ted. Anyway I never said knickers to the librarian. They are all old and ugly, who cares about their knickers.'

'Well maybe "tits", which they heard it as "nits",' said Archie, whose Officer vocabulary ranged around bums and tits.

Archie continued, 'Well, I'll text Stephen, he's a retired English teacher. He'll know what the n word is.'

'Well, try now, before he's deep in his cups,' said Ted.

A text message came back immediately from Stephen.

'Ted must have called the librarian a "nigger". The "n" word is a nigger, banned in the UK and the USA.'

'I never called the librarian a nigger. Why should I, she was just an ordinary Scotswoman,' said Ted.

'Are you sure she wasn't a bit dark? She looked a bit dark to me,' said Archie.

'The lights were low over where the librarians work,' said Ted. 'I never called her a nigger, I never spoke to her.'

'*Racial hatred*, it says so in this letter they have sent you,' said Archie, looking severely at Ted, and pressing the letter to his chest. You were carrying my philosophy books, the black boy pushed into you. What did you say?'

'I said, *how nice to meet you, where are you from?*'

'Wait,' said Archie. 'I will phone Stephen again.'

Stephen apologised profusely.

'The new "n" word is "nice", a cliché, banal, not to be used in front of children. You will have to go to the course revising your vocabulary.'

'That should be nice,' said Ted. 'Opoos.'

# TOFF'S BOTTLE

Archie banged on Ted's door. A ferret face appeared, followed by a thin body in a brown fur dressing gown. Archie said, 'My sister has sent me this invitation to the Conservative Party Garden Party. She says it's time I met a better class of person.'

'But you know me,' said Ted.

'A better class, a better class,' said Archie, grinding his stick in the landing floor.

'Tories,' said Ted. 'Like the dossers at the Stock Exchange, the fixers, and swindlers at the bank, the tarts at Ascot, Boris Johnston, Berlington Bertie, Champagne Charlie, and all the lot.'

'Champagne Charlie. Wooster and Jeeves. Of course, Ted, you will go as my servant, to open the champers.'

Archie found a smoking jacket and bow tie in Age Concern Charity Shop. He poked about with his stick in the skip outside and yanked out some dungarees and a cloth cap for Ted to wear. The pair went off to the Garden Party, Archie brandishing his stick and Ted his bottle opener.

They saw Caroline at the gate. She gave a social smile under the wide-brimmed hat and extended a gloved hand.

'How fat you are, Archie,' said the kind sister and then noticing Ted she said, 'Why have you brought a window cleaner with you?'

'He's Edward, my servant. He's here to pour out the champagne.'

'How strange. Catering has been supplied by the Dorchester.'

Another lady tapped Caroline on the shoulder, and she bounded off, anticipation oozing from her body.

Archie and Ted went into the garden which radiated millions of pounds. A waiter appeared on the manicured lawn, but seeing Ted veered away with his tray of drinks.

'Here, my man,' shouted Archie after him.

Doubtfully, the waiter approached.

'This man', said Archie, pointing to Ted, 'is to open my bottle.'

'I don't understand,' said the waiter, in faltering English.

'It's the Toff's bottle, Champers,' said Archie.

'I'll make enquiries,' said the cringing foreigner.

Soon a bevy of penguins appeared disputing in high incomprehensible tones. One carried a bottle. He said, 'Toff's bottle, for Mr Johnson?'

A loud speaker hailed.

Boris Johnson appeared, his hair joyful in the summer breeze. A TV crew was beside him.

Archie pushed Ted forward. Ted was given the bottle and the bottle opener.

'Are you a Londoner?' asked Boris.

'Old Kent Road,' said Ted doffing his cap.

'Fine,' said Boris. He put his arm around Ted in front of the camera. The journalists crowded round for the shot. Archie was in the picture too.

Caroline's loud mouth could be heard saying, 'I brought them here to meet a better class of person.'

Byee Archie and Ted.

# TYPING NUDE

'Look what it says in the reference for No.5.'

Stephen Love's face was a strange mixture of horror and joy, like a sparking unfathomable pool. Stephen Love, the junior solicitor and the administrative officer, Mrs Jones, were reading the references for the post of Solicitors' Typist at Best Choices—Legal and Financial Services, Aberdeen.

Mrs Jones read out the line which Stephen had pointed to,

'Sometimes types nude on her own initiative'. The reference was from the City Council.

'Well', she said, unfazed, 'they have some strange policies there. Dressing down days and so on. I've seen staff with red noses, carrying buckets come out of the Town House. It's all left-wing politics.'

Mrs Jones dismissed further discussion of the reference for No. 5. She wanted to finish the selection task in time to be able to use her flexi card to meet her children from school.

'We'll call up No. 5 to interview,' said Stephen Love 'She's the best qualified and most interesting, and write to a couple of the others too, to balance things. I'm sure I will find what I want.'

'I'll see the letters of invitation go out. The interviews will be next Thursday at 10 a.m. as the Personnel Department has decided,' said Mrs Jones, and she grabbed her coat from the stand.

It was next Thursday. Miss Deidre Brown sat down elegantly, keeping her legs together.

*Brown by name, brown by dress, brown hair, and brown eyes*, thought Mrs Jones.

Mr Love, however, was watching her body move under her dress, hips, and breasts.

Mrs Jones perceived a drop at the end of Miss Brown's long nose. Her voice was hoarse. Stephen Love was reminded of cigarettes, and night clubs, drink fuelled, rank desire.

The application form said Miss Brown was 39 years old. When she had left, Mrs Jones commented she looked older. Stephen Love said inaudibly, 'Jealous women.' She lived alone. *Spinster,* Mrs Jones thought. *No ties,* Stephen thought. She lived near the Harbour, Stephen and Mrs Jones looked at each other. Pictures of short skirts and drunken leers came into Stephen's mind.

Mrs Jones found from the interview that Deidre Brown had very good typing qualifications and an excellent knowledge of Excel, Database, the Internet, and the Intranet. There was no reason not to appoint her.

Mrs Jones asked the standard question about why the candidate wished to move from her present post. Ms Brown said she thought she would have more scope to act on her own initiative in a private company.

'Well, you'll be mostly working for me,' said Stephen. 'So that's fine. I like women, I mean staff to take their own initiatives.'

Mrs Jones looked at her nails and posed the next standard question.

'And what are your out-of-work hobbies and interests, Miss Brown?'

'I was told at the Council that those questions are not in line with anti-discriminatory policies.'

'Really!' said Stephen. *Anti-discriminatory policies, what interests?* he thought.

The interview was over.

'We'll let you know, said Mrs Jones, as she grabbed for her coat.

Deidre Brown was appointed to work at Best Choices at Stephen Love's request. On the day she started, Mrs Jones found her a seat in the General Office facing a sliding glass pane which looked on to the Junior Solicitor's Office, where Stephen Love had a desk. When Deidre Brown was seated, Stephen Love moved his desk, as he found it was uneven on the floor. He could watch her through the glass pane. Ms Brown slid the pane to take the documents from his hand, and he could see the rise and fall of her breasts as she moved to receive them. In the periods when he was 'thinking' about his work, he looked up to admire the curve of Ms Brown's back. As he strained upward to get his top coat from the coat stand, he saw Ms Brown's legs, swinging as if to music.

The partner, Mr Lloyd came into the office. He leant over and said in Stephen Love's ear, 'What dull women Mrs Jones appoints as typists. Perhaps they are bursting with sex inside. Perhaps it's the beauties, like Marion, in our office, who are ice all the way through.'

'Some have a reputation,' said Stephen archly.

'Our female staff! Dull as ditch water,' said Lloyd.

The Marion of whom Lloyd spoke had been Stephen's only live-in girlfriend to date. They had been the same age, now 26 and both Junior Solicitors. Marion was a career woman and their life at home had been one long law seminar, contract law, employment law, the law relating to abandoned children, etc. He had told his friend, Ron, he had gone to bed with Best Choices not a girl. His sexual nature had been thwarted and remained dormant, waiting for that gentle tap which would wake him from his sleep and turn him in to that rampant sexual being he knew he was.

Alone in his functional two-bedroom flat in crowded Kepplestone, a young professional dormitory development, Stephen opened up his laptop and caressed its purring keys. He drank a large whiskey and the ghost of a female hand touched the keys and moved with his. Their fingers intertwined, to play music of love. His hand moved from the laptop to bare, inviting legs. As he drank another whiskey, a nude female bottom appeared on his lap and long breasts fell forward to touch the keys. The words appeared on the screen in **Bold** 20 *Lets Make Love*. The vision faded. Stephen collapsed on his bed and dreamt the dream of the future, while gentle keys tapped a love song, and the body, not yet acquired, visited by proxy.

The following day, Stephen went to Best Choices. He sat at his desk and his hand trembled as he opened the post. Aware still of his guilty night, he looked through the pane and saw the brown outline of Deidre Brown; brown hair tied back, moisture on the end of her long nose back straight, typing. She hit the keys as if they were naughty boys. Her prim mouth seemed to move to the pain, and yet sweet scent wafted on the air, heralding desire.

Stephen got up and moved awkwardly to the door of the typing pool. He stood there for several minutes. Mrs Jones said,

'Can we help you Stephen?'

He moved to Deidre Brown's workstation and gazed at her like a devotee at Lourdes would at the shrine of Bernadette.

'Is everything all right?' asked Mrs Jones. 'Miss Brown's work meets your standard?'

'Yes,' said Stephen, in the same exalted mood. 'Yes' and he put his hand over Deidre Brown's and clasped it.

The other typists' expressions were encouraging the joke, set up they believe by the young solicitors.

Then they watched as Stephen knelt by Deidre Brown's work station and implored

'Will you come to dinner with me tonight at the Caledonian Hotel, at 8 p.m.?'

'How kind,' said Deidre Brown.

Stephen left the typing pool.

Mrs Jones said,

'You're being set up, Deidre. It's an office joke, or he wants to get information from you about the business.'

But Deidre knew he had been watching her. She knew it was love. She felt young again.

At 8 p.m. prompt, Stephen appeared at the table he had reserved in the Caledonian dining room. He had bulge in his trousers. Deidre saw him, blushed and patted her hair.

The bulge was an engagement ring, which he removed, and stammering with emotion said to Deidre,

'Will you mar-mar-marry me? Or I will go mad.' He gave her the ring.

'How very kind,' said Deidre Brown. Office joke or not, she thought, she would keep him to it. She put the ring in her handbag and clicked it shut.

'I will go to the Registrar's Office and get the papers tomorrow. Soon we will be married.'

'How nice,' said Deidre Brown. 'I hope I will give satisfaction.'

Stephen reeled away from the table, and out through the restaurant door. The other diners thought him drunk. Deidre Brown finished her dinner.

The following day Stephen walked to the Registrar's Office to obtain the necessary papers and information needed for his marriage to Deidre Brown.

He decided to call in at the Town House at lunchtime and visit his friend who worked in the Law and Administration Department. Ron suggested they should go to lunch.

During the first course, the two young solicitors talked about the pros and cons of their respective employment, then as the sweet course came, Stephen Love asked casually,

'Was there anything unusual about the typist Deidre Brown who came to us from you?'

'No, not at all,' said Ron, a little surprised. 'She was competent. She saw the newsletter came out. She typed it on her own initiative. We were very pleased.'

'Typed news? On her own initiative?' said Stephen, who, to Ron, seemed inexplicably downcast by this information.

'Yes, to be frank, Stephen, a lot of our typists are hopeless, and no one has the time to check the copy or read it through. It goes out full of errors. We've had some real howlers, most embarrassing, but Deidre Brown was competent. An older woman, you know. Why do you ask?'

'Just rumours,' said Stephen.

'Rumours about Deidre Brown? I'm surprised,' said Ron.

Stephen walked back to his office slowly. She had typed news for the newsletter. She was a spinster typist of 40, plain as a pikestaff. He was engaged to her.

She had never typed nude.

# U OR NON U

## An English Suburb 1963

'Have you seen what that Crowte next door has put in his garden?' Portly, red-faced Commander English was shouting at his wife, Hermione.

'Well, yes, dear,' she said, 'there's an ornament by a little pool.'

'A gnome, a plastic gnome!' her husband replied 'We have the house on the market. We need a good price. That plastic gnome will put a stop to that. It drags the Close down, like all the net curtains that have been put up and plastic flowers in the windows, and flying ducks on the walls. It's so lower middle class, so banal.'

'Now, dear, don't get so worked up, or you'll go the way of your brother. It's only a little gnome with a fishing rod. It can't do too much harm.'

'It shows this is an area with poor taste. People ought to have to get planning permission for that kind of thing. I'll tell old Smithers, it's his job as MP to get the law changed. Then I'll send the Crowte a solicitor's letter—that's if he reads English.'

'Why don't you just go and have a quiet word with him? I think things are always best settled that way,' said Hermione.

'I'll go now,' said Commander English, and he marched off and up his neighbours path, giving the gnome a look of great disgust as he passed the garden.

'Ja?' an elderly man came to the door.

'It's the gnome,' Commander English came to the point straight away with naval precision.

The elderly man, Herr Deutsch, looked puzzled.

'It's the gnome. I demand you remove it. It lowers the tone of the Close.' Commander English advanced on the elderly foreigner, and jabbed him in the chest with his finger.

'That gnome could take £500 off the price of my house.'

Mr Deutsch looked even more puzzled.

'Warum?'

'War what?' asked Commander English, angrier still.

'Vy should £500 off your house, because of my gnome? He magician?'

'It stands for bad taste. People will think the people in the Close have no breeding, come from bad back grounds, no taste, education,' said the Commander.

'Bad taste?' said Herr Deutsh. 'I show you gnomes are in the highest taste. You come in, I show you my display.'

Mr Deutsh politely opened the front door. The Commander followed, anxious to see the interior of Mr Deutsch house.

Mr Deusch led him into a back room. Heavy curtains were drawn and the room was dark. The walls seemed to be brown and unevenly painted, like a grotto. Mr Deutsch turned on the lights and a row of red bulbs illuminated a series of wide, rising shelves. The effect was to draw the viewer forward into the grotto.

The shelves were filled with gnomes. The oldest gnome, a 'gobbi' and its female mate, leered down fearfully. Below it was shelved a 'Daemon' and then a gnome of terracotta clay. There were elegant models from famous potteries, Dresden, Wedgwood.

On the shelves sentimental gnomes mirrored the play of figures from Society, fishing, dancing, playing cards, and gnomes playing roles which graced the home and set the tone of domesticity. There was a copy of a grotto of gnomes designed for the visit of the Prince of Wales on Long Island in 1920.

Commander English was mesmerized. It seemed that in the past gnomes had been the symbol of aristocracy, property, wealth, and education. He looked at each gnome separately. Never had he seen such a collection.

He had travelled the world in the Navy, and he engaged Herr Deutsch in conversation. Soon they were in the kitchen making coffee together and pouring over other memorabilia of the German, and over his collection of books.

Herr Deutsch told the Commander of local press interest in his collection, and that there would be articles and photos in tomorrow's edition of the *Chronical*.

The Commander returned and told the wife of his morning of marvels. He was now determined to go to the auctions and sales and start a collection himself.

'But don't put it in the garden,' said Hermione with a smile.

The following morning, the local paper rattled through the door. Commander English grabbed it and turned to the section *Homes and Gardens*. The display about Herr Deutsch collection was tasteful and interesting.

Herr Deutsch had put several gnomes in the garden and a crowd gathered of people who had read the article.

'What a cultured neighbourhood,' said an American.

'And the house next door is for sale,' said another.

Commander English was offered £300 over his asking price for his house. He decided he could find nowhere better to live or with such delightful and interesting neighbours.

# A NIGHT OF LOVE

'Oh, it's you. You're back, Mandy. I was beginning to worry about you. Did you sleep over at Emma's?'

'No, Mum.'

'Didn't you go to *News.*'

'No, Mum. Katie's sandal broke. We wanted a drink, and we were right by this dark Club place, so we went in there. It was full of old men, really old men, 40 or 50 years old. The women in there were like the teachers we had at Northfield. It was quite dark, and there were posters about festivals and things on the walls. There was a man on the stage, with dreadlocks, shouting. He sounded dead vicious, like Dad when he used to live with us. Then he finished and another man went to the microphone. He was thin, old, with long dirty blond hair, and a blue scarf round his neck. He put his hand over the microphone and sort of pipped, like little bubbles of air were coming out of him and dissolving into the air. Emma said to me, "Ain't there no music? This is 'orrible, let's go and find somewhere where there is a bit of life." Katie said she would go with Emma to the Ladies and try and fix her sandal, and then we'd go.

'I sat there on my own, and this next man came to the stage, punching with his voice like he hated us. I hoped the girls would come back soon. Then this wrinkly came and sat down by me and started to talk to me. He was quite nice really. He asked me all about myself, what school I had been to, what job I did, what music I liked, stuff like that. He seemed really interested, not like Dad. He looked at me intently, and smiled into my face. Then he picked up a bit of my hair and said it was like the sun's rays. Emma and Katie didn't come back. I suppose they had seen me with him and thought I'd clicked, so they left me.

'He seemed to know all about wine, so he said he would teach me. He brought me three glasses, and said the colour rising in my cheeks was like a hopeful dawn.

'I said, "You talk like the books we had at school. GCSE and that." He said he was a writer.'

'A writer?' said Mum.

'Yes, he asked me if I would like to see the abode of his humble muse. I didn't know what he meant, but it seemed I was stuck with him, even though he was so old, so I said OK.

'I'd had a bit too much to drink, so he put his arm round me, and helped me out of the Club and down the road. We got along the pavement to this old van, which he said was his faithful steed, and he helped me in. There was a lot of electronic equipment in the back, and books thrown in on top of it. I said I was going to be sick. He said it was only a little way. He stopped in Rosemount Place, and we went into this tenement. The lobby was dirt, full of old papers strewn about. He helped me go up the steps, there were thousands of them, winding round and round, like in one of them old castles. At the top there was just this black door. He said it was his. It was like a sort of attic inside. Full of books, and these posters on the wall, like the ones in that Club. There was no furniture in the living room, just these big cushions, red and black. There was a picture of a nude woman on the wall, with a pot on her head. There was as statue of another nude woman on a small table, with a snake round her.

'Then he came heavy on me, pushing off my coat, grasping me and moaning on about nubile nymphs. He said I was like a moonbeam come from eternity to lighten his dark soul. He said we would unite and go to the edge of Paradise, and then he pushed me roughly into the bedroom.'

I said, 'You're not my boyfriend. I don't even know your name.

'He bit my face and said, "Harry Naylor, now at your service," and threw me on the bed. The bed was black, black sheets, black duvet. I could see the curtains were dirty, and there were papers and notebooks all over the floor. He tore at my clothes and said I was his harvest, ripe corn for the plucking. He said he would devour me and take me to heaven in his belly.

'Then he started licking and moaning and doing things.'

'Men always do things, Mandy,' said her mother. 'Did you have sex with him?'

'I was there all night, Mum, I thought he would never stop. I was fed up with him.'

'Have you been taking the pill?'

'No, I stopped after Jack.'

'Well, it will have to be a termination. Dave will leave me, if there's a baby here.'

'Oh, Mum.'

'Are you seeing him again?'

'No, he says his life's over and he is going into a void.'

'He's going where?'

'A void, Mum.'

'What did you say his name was?'

'Harry Naylor. He says he's a writer.'

'Is he on the telly?'

# ANGELS DON'T SMELL

'She's 'orrible. She's like our classroom assistant. She's got great 'orrible yellow teeth. Her fur's all stuck together. She smells.'

'Mandy, she's your cousin. Ninety-seven per cent of her genes are the same as yours. She's a little girl like you. You're both descended from Australopithecus. I showed you the coloured chart of the monkeys and apes. The evolutionary tree leads up to you and to her,' said Jerry, father and microbiology PhD student.

'She's like the wolf in my picture book about Red Riding Hood. She's got a nasty white dress on. She's showing all her horrible hairy legs. She's got an 'orrible hat, like an old woman. She smells.'

'Now, Mandy, she's your cousin. I brought you here specially to see her,' said Jerry.

'I want a lollipop,' said Mandy, diverted from the chimps by the sight of a brightly coloured sweet stand opposite.

'OK, Mandy, we'll go and buy one,' said Jerry, and he sauntered over the path, swinging Mandy by the hand.

When they had brought the red-and-green lollipop, Jerry steered Mandy back to the Chimp- House.

'Look at her,' said Jerry 'She drinks from a cup just like a human.' Mandy pressed her face against the cage.

A brown fur arm darted through the bars.

'She's taken my pop. I hate her. She's taken my pop,' said Mandy, tears coming to her eyes. 'I hate her.' She stamped her feet.

The chimp was sitting on her red plastic chair, a rogue smile on her face, as she licked the pop.

'I hate her. She smells like the bottom of a wheelie bin. She stole my pop,' the child screamed.

Jerry looked at the chimp, entranced. 'She looks human. See how she licks that lollipop.'

'She's a thief. I can't stand her smell.'

Jerry steered Mandy away from the cage.

'We'll go home now, Mummy will be expecting us.'

Mandy left her tears behind in the Zoo, and on the way home she asked Jerry,

'Why didn't you come to see the school play? I was an angel. Angels wear pretty clothes. I had a gold dress, and a ribbon in my hair, with pretty white flowers. Why didn't you come?'

'Mummy wanted you to go to that school, not me,' said Daddy Jerry.

'Daddy,' Mandy persisted, swinging Jerry's arm, 'angels are pretty. Angels have nice clothes. Angels don't smell.'

'Angels don't smell!' said Jerry. 'Who says angels don't smell?'

*    *    *

Next day was Christmas Eve.

Mummy Karen said, 'Surely you're not going to the Lab today Jerry? It's Christmas Eve. We're going to your brother's house tomorrow. We must get ready.'

'I am going to get ready,' said Jerry, with a sneaky grin.

*   *   *

It was Christmas Day, and the family was driving to Jerry's brother's house. Jerry pressed down on the accelerator, a wicked smile on his face. 'Angels don't smell,' he leered. 'Angels don't smell!'

'Whatever do you mean?" asked Mummy Karen. 'Drive more slowly or we'll all be with the angels.'

Finally, they arrived at Dave and Jane's house.

When Dave let them in, Jane was in the front room, dressing the tree.

'I'll put the angel on the tree, Jane,' said Jerry.

'What, you've brought Christmas decorations? You have? I thought you didn't believe in any of the Jesus nonsense,' said Dave.

Jerry went up to the tree and placed a cardboard angel at the top. Then, without being seen, he lit the tail of the angel with a cigarette lighter.

'Oh, it's like the bottom of a wheelie bin,' said Jane. 'What a dreadful smell!'

The angel then sped off the tree and onto the floor, like a firework, and only a burnt piece of card remained.

Mandy watched, eyes popping. Jerry turned to her.

'She's a fossil fuel, carbon. Now go and play with your cousins!'

**Elizabeth Reinach 2.4.09**

# THE PROFESSOR AND
# THE CLEANER

The grey antiquity of the University buildings, lost in the heights of learning, merged into the misty dawn. The building stood as yet, unpopulated. The No. 6

bus disgorged an army of the dawn, cackling with the early-morning birds, fat-striped in plebeian overalls. Contract cleaners, employed to clean the surfaces of the University, to scrub pollution from its face.

Professor Flavian Fitzlaird swung into the senior car park at 8.30 a.m. and made his way to the complex modern structure, housing the Sociology Department, where the insect life of social man was dissected.

The Professor had forgotten that he had to teach the third year course Gender and Class that day. Boredom had cast a dense cloud over his memory, given a jolt only at breakfast, when he glanced at his week planner.

'Oh damn,' he said to himself. 'Well the notes from last year's lecture are in my desk at the Department. I can go in and read them through by ten.'

At 8.45 a.m., Flavian navigated himself through the complex anonymous security of the Social Science building. His number was 007, he wryly observed.

The cleaner was still there in his office.

*Oh well, it doesn't matter about her,* he thought as he started to rummage through his desk.

Then he looked up.

*How odd. How extraordinary she looks,* he said to himself as the cleaner was preparing to go.

She was oblong, and in her stained pink overall, looked like an ill-painted door. She was short, maybe 5' 3". Her hair was dyed a blondish brown, and it seemed as if a dead rat had been implanted on the top. The hair hung at the side in two uneven bunches. Her dark-blue eyes were slanted, very moist. They slithered about like a dank unfathomable pool. Her skin was an unhealthy pallor, merging into moist pink lip gloss. Flavian supposed she was in her forties.

'Hello,' he said, but she did not reply. She was staring at him. Perhaps she is thinking, 'Shiny bald head, like a dirty hazelnut, long inquisitive nose, dry mouth. *Perhaps my face is repulsive to her*, thought Flavian. He returned to rummage in his desk drawer for his notes, and he felt her slide away.

The academic day droned on, merging with the evening reception for post-graduate students. Flavian was obliged to attend. He feigned enthusiasm for the students' choice of thesis subjects, *Existential Approach to Gender Choice*. 'Oh, well done, I will be interested to read your outline'. New *Conceptions in Social Class Classification*. 'Oh, that will be of real value to the subject'. He avoided the cheap wine and crisps, and fabricated an excuse to leave at 8 p.m. He drove home to the boredom of his flat, filled with antiques and 'good pictures'. With distaste, he picked up his latest draft book, with the intention of proofreading. His thoughts drifted off.

'That extraordinary cleaner, she should be painted by a Picasso disciple. In a social survey, she would receive the code SEG d/e, part-time employed, living on a G estate. Poor lady.'

Flavian had been divorced for many years. He saw his adult children only occasionally. His last relationship, three years ago, had convinced him he had nothing more to give. He was a dead man, dead to Sociology, dead to women.

He had set his alarm clock for an hour before he usually got up, a mistake unconsciously made. He had no classes that morning. He knew he should work on the paper he was to deliver at the Cambridge Seminar later that month,

'Income differences in marriage with part-time workers in different social classes', but his mouth felt dry and his hand shook. *Perhaps I will drive to the University and look at the post*, he thought.

He arrived at 8.30 a.m. again. The cleaner was there. She was looking at his shelves, when he came in. The books were mainly seminal sociology texts and more modern books on marriage and class. There were five copies of his most recent book on the lower shelf. He was convinced the cleaner had withdrawn one to read. She was putting it back hurriedly.

For some reason he did not understand he said, 'I'm sorry.'

She turned and he swam in her moist gaze. Her pink mouth opened like a fish. Then she turned, duster in hand.

He walked to the shelves. The book was balanced on the edge. He was sure it had been taken out and hastily put back. He took it out and placed it on a chair near the door.

He now felt he had no further reason to stay at the University. Soon his colleagues would be arriving. The academic chitchat, the barely concealed malice and envy, did not offend him; it just bored him. His post was open on the table. Three invitations to speak at Conferences, one on a Television programme. He could deal with those later. He decided to go to town.

Clothes, he needed clothes. He brought a polo neck sweater from Burtons and continued down the street. A pink garment winked at him from a shop called *Harman's Uniforms and Overalls*. He walked past, but a magnet seemed to draw him back. Returning to the shop, the pink garment seemed to wink at him. It was the kind of overall the cleaner wore. It winked again, invitingly, sexily. *How extraordinary*, he thought. It seemed to follow him down the road.

There was a faculty meeting in the afternoon. Polite barbs, belittling thrusts sparred over a pointless agenda. Flavian felt the thirty years of his academic life condense into that one hour of alienation. The grey towers of his early hopes receded; he stood alone in empty success.

The following day, he had to meet a postgraduate student. He wandered through the maze of the Sociology building, arriving in his office at 9 a.m. The cleaner had gone, as had the book. The office had been locked all day yesterday. He was certain the cleaner had taken his book. He felt a haze of pleasure. He had never been pleased by academic recognition, hollow praise from hollow men. But the thought of the cleaner reading his book filled him with pride. Perhaps she would find wisdom and solace in *Dysfunctions of Class and Their Impact on Gender Mobility.*

The postgraduate student was female, bright, pretty, and deferential. She wore a short skirt and sat with her legs crossed. He was irritated by her presence. All the girl students irritated him. Little Miss Piggies wriggling along in tight jeans, plaits, and ponytails.

That afternoon he met the new first year. Twenty boys and girls from privileged backgrounds, who had opted for Sociology, either as a filler course or as an ignorant desire to be social workers. A sudden thought flashed in Flavian's head.

'We'll go on a field trip' he said to the students 'We'll get the bus to go to Eastfields Estate. I want you to get a flavour of the life there. Observe the vandalism, the walk up flats, the type of shops. It will be good background for your first year studies.' Field trips had never been undertaken by the first year before. The class were enthusiastic. A day out.

Two boys insisted on driving their cars and took some of the other students as passengers. The rest boarded the No. 6 bus. Flavian gazed out along the route. They met up at the small shopping precinct. Flavian pointed out the lack of any shops which were not Bookies, off-licenses, and fast food shops, and he told the students that these were indictors defining the life style of the estate. Flavian then led the students up the hill, past weed-infested open spaces, where arms and legs of amputated furniture lay. He pointed to the architecture, the walk-up flats, and the penitential stone stairs. The students, believing themselves clever, filled their notebooks with cliches 'god-forsaken' 'forgotten' 'smell of despair'. Then Flavian saw her. She was at the window of an upper flat, gazing down on him. Neither she or he waved, but their gazes locked.

Flavian told the students to make their way back to the University and write a report on *Life Style on a G level Housing Estate*. He told them he had to go to town and would be taking a different bus.

A thought flashed into Flavian's mind that he should spend the evening cleaning up his flat. Perhaps an overall would keep his clothes clean. He alighted in the high street at the stop by *Harman's Overalls and Uniforms*. As he looked in the window he started to feel his hands grow clammy. With a heart beating with excitement, he entered the shop and picked out a pink overall in size XL. He paid for it with his Credit Card, and carried it home as if it were a precious object. Without waiting for the evening, he put it on like a girl would try on a dress in breathless anticipation of a date. He located the hoover. Busy, happy, calm, he cleaned until perhaps 9 p.m. Perhaps he would do some more cleaning tomorrow.

At 9.30 p.m., the phone rang. It was David Eastman, the Professor of Sociology at another University. His academic interests were close to Flavian's.

'Flavian', he said, 'I agreed to go on the ITV discussion programme tonight, *Changes in Modern Marriage*. They invited you first, and said you did not reply. I was of course a second choice. Have you been at a Conference? Doesn't your secretary keep you informed? They were surprised they got no reply from you.'

'I don't know,' said Flavian. 'There must have been some mix-up. I don't remember receiving the invitation. Anyway, I'm sure you're a better choice than me. Certainly more telegenic. When's it on? I'll see it.'

'It's coming on now, at 10 p.m. We recorded it this afternoon,' said David.

Flavian put on the television. The programme was of the question-and-answer variety. The camera flashed round the audience. Then Flavian saw her, the cleaner, sitting on the second row. His heart missed a beat. He switched the television off.

He was convinced she had taken the invitation. She must have thought he would be on the panel and booked a place in the audience. Flavian could feel his tension mounting. Had she really wished to see him? Or was she just a television groupie?

Flavian slept fitfully. In his dreams he was fighting his way out of a television box. A pink overall was on the line. He tried to grab it. The box was closed. The Principal floated towards the box and became a tiny peg on the line, fastening the overall.

Flavian finally woke at 6.30 a.m. and jumped out of bed. Frantically, he dressed and drove his car at an illegal pace to the University. The cleaners were being disgorged from the No.6 bus. He could see her. He drove round and round the University, like a cat chasing its tail.

Two of his colleagues, who were preparing for a breakfast with the business community, saw him and phoned security. His car was stopped and he was gently guided into his office, to calm down.

At 9 a.m., his secretary found him pacing in his office, laughing to himself. She was too deferential to ask him what was the matter, so she brought him some tea and the internal post.

Flavian sat in his chair, pretending to read the memoranda. Then his eyes fixed themselves on Item 10 of The University Administrative Committee meeting minutes.

The Awarding of the Cleaning Contract.

It has been decided not to reward the cleaning contract for the University to *Local Clean*, as the bid has been undercut by *Irons Europe*, a Polish firm who will employ Polish migrant cleaners, after they have been fully vetted.'

Flavian fell off his chair, his dead weight dragging him to the floor. The secretary came in for the teacup. She knew now she must act. She called the Student Medical Services, and within fifteen minutes, the doctor was in Flavian's office. The two colleagues were now back from the Business Breakfast, and they and the secretary told the doctor what they had seen of Flavian's behaviour that morning.

Flavian was admitted to the local mental hospital as a voluntary patient. His sympathetic psychiatrist recommended a change of career, at least for a while. Flavian never returned to the Chair of Sociology at the University. His former colleagues were unsure of his present employment.

Printed in the United States
By Bookmasters